LITTLE TREE THAT CRIED

A TOUCHING TALE FOR ALL AGES

BY: CLARENCE B. PARKER
ILLUSTRATED BY: JIMMY BLINN

Published by
Clarence B. Parker

Printed by CreateSpace

Copyright © 2014 Clarence B. Parker
All rights reserved.

ISBN: 1452808600
ISBN 13: 9781452808604

DEDICATION

To my wife, Lucy, and to you, the reader.

You may read this story in quiet solitude; or, you may be blessed to read this to a child, grandchild or great-grandchild sitting on your lap. Whichever, enjoy and embrace the diminishing sounds of pages being turned.

A SPECIAL ACKNOWLEDGEMENT

A special thank you to Jimmy Blinn for being a sounding board and supporter of this text. Jimmy has displayed the professional approach in formatting and providing the outstanding free-lance illustrations displayed throughout this story.

THE
LITTLE TREE
THAT CRIED

(FINALLY, THE REAL STORY)

GREETINGS FROM THE AUTHOR

Have you ever considered that trees have feelings similar to people?

Yes, trees are alive. They give off oxygen, consume a lot of water and receive nutrients from many of the same chemicals we do.

A tree is sensitive to sunshine, rainfall, lightning, heat, cold and floods.

A tree provides shelter and is a food source for birds and animals. Trees have a life span. Trees have feelings.

One particular tree, the evergreen, populated the earth long before man existed. Today there are evergreen species that are over three thousand years old and *still* growing. Some tower over three hundred feet in height and are *still* growing.

Consider the amazing stories these aged giants of the forest would tell if they could speak.

Life's journey for trees is arduous, but a gratifying one.

This writing is a journey of trees speaking and expressing their feelings and emotions. Whether you are a child or an adult, I know you will be touched by this story

~ The Author

PROLOGUE

This is a true story. Well, the facts are real. The main characters are trees and not people.

Trees are among the most plentiful and largest plants on earth. They are also different from most other living things in another way: They never stop growing as long as they live. They do not come and go with the seasons like flowers and farm crops.

In the United States there are over a thousand kinds of trees. Two of the types are in general categories. One category is called the needle-leaf tree. The second category is the broad-leaf.

Most needle-leaf trees are fir, pine, hemlock, spruce and cedar. They have needles that cling to the branches year-round. For this reason, the trees are always green and called evergreens.

The broad-leaf trees have broad flat leaves. Most broad-leaf trees shed their leaves in the autumn of the year. They are called deciduous (d-sid-u-us).

This story centers on fir-evergreen trees. Fir-evergreen trees are commonly called Christmas trees.

Nine types of firs grow in the United States. Two types grow in the East and seven in the mountains of the West. Balsam firs are common in the East. The Douglas fir and the red fir dominate in the West.

All fifty states grow evergreen trees.

The origin of the first Christmas tree used as decoration occurred in Germany during the sixteenth century. The first use of Christmas trees in America was in the eighteenth century.

Evergreens have long been a symbol of life. The early Romans celebrated prosperity by decorating their homes with greenery. Egyptians brought palm tree fronds into the home to symbolize life.

The word Christmas comes from the early English phrase "Cristes Maesse" which means "Christ's Mass." The event is celebrated as the birthday of Jesus Christ. No one knows exactly when Jesus was born. The date December 25th was established around 350 A.D. by a bishop in Rome. He ordered the people to use this date as the Feast of Saturn and celebrate the birthday of the sun. Near the same time, early Christians used December 25th as the birthday of Jesus.

Are you ready?

Okay, let us begin and take an evergreen tree journey.

Table of Contents

	GREETINGS FROM THE AUTHOR	ix
	PROLOGUE	xi
1	THE JOURNEY BEGINS	1
2	DECISION TIME	4
3	THE WORD IS OUT	5
4	ON TO THE FARM	7
5	LIFE ON THE FARM	8
6	HARVEST OPERATIONS	10
7	YEAR END NEARS	12
8	A SPECIAL CHRISTMAS	13
9	THE SOBERING YEARS	16
10	MATURING	18
11	SILENT NIGHT COUNTDOWN	20
12	SPECIAL TREATMENT	22
13	THE PARTING BEGINS	24
14	SHIPPING OUT	26
15	BONDAGE	28
16	EXISTING - BARELY	30
17	GIVE THANKS	32
18	BUSY DAY	34
19	THE TIME FACTOR	36
20	A DARK DAY	38
21	ON THE CLOCK	40
22	A GIVEN WORD	42
23	A PERFECT SETTING	47
24	THE AFTERWORD	50
	TREE TRIVIA TID-BITS	55
	ABOUT THE AUTHOR	57
	ABOUT THE ILLUSTRATOR	59

1
THE JOURNEY BEGINS

I am a Douglas fir evergreen tree. My siblings tell me I was born in a local tree nursery. The nursery used seeds from fir cones to bring us to life.

When the fir cones mature, the cones drop from the limbs of the mother tree. With time, the cones shed their scales within which the seeds are enclosed. Each cone has many seeds.

My nursery green house, number 11, had green tinted glass walls and roof. Each greenhouse provided ideal growing conditions for thousands of baby seedlings.

Green houses are nurseries for seedling trees of different ages and stages of growth.

I vaguely remember the daily care of the nurserymen. They were all dedicated to their tasks. There was one special man. He was elderly and stooped, with long white hair. He had a kind smile, was soft spoken and whistled catchy tunes. He would speak to the seedlings with encouraging comments.

"How's my little family doing? Straighten up little one. Always stand tall." He was a happy and kind man.

2
DECISION TIME

Life was so good. The green house nursery provided for all of the seedlings needs. Time was spent growing, relaxing and being coddled by the nursery workers.

After nearly four years, the tender loving care helped their roots grow strong and become established in the fertile soil. Most seedlings were nearly nine inches tall at this time.

The maturing seedlings knew that "baby-sitting-time" was nearing an end. Recent activities in several near-by greenhouses created anxious whispering that evergreens were being selected for varying futures and transferred to other locations.

The answer would come soon. On one cool morning, nursery workers entered greenhouse number 11 and attached colored labels to many of the planting trays. Some trays had orange labels and some had yellow labels.

The little seedlings' tray had an orange label. The little trees had no idea what the label meant.

3
THE WORD IS OUT

The elderly white-haired nursery man entered green-house number 11 with two of his assistants.

They walked slowly between the stacked rows of planting trays.

In a soft voice, the elderly man spoke and gestured his instructions.

"Tomorrow, assist in the shipping of all trays with a yellow label to the State Reforestation Department."

He paused, "Treat them *royally*. They will become our future forests."

With that, loud cheers of, ***"I'm number ONE"***, echoed through the green-house.

Because evergreen trees can only vocally communicate with other evergreens, the joyous sounds were never heard by the elderly man and his assistants.

The old man spoke again, "Ship all the seedling trays marked with the orange labels to Christmas Tree Farms in Happy Valley."

The words Christmas Tree Farms and Happy Valley were first met with a stunned silence. Then suddenly the seedlings erupted into happy cheers.

"We're going to be Christmas trees!"
They were all so happy!

4
ON TO THE FARM

Trays with thousands of seedlings were loaded on a flatbed truck and driven slowly to The Happy Valley Christmas Tree Farms. The journey lasted less than two hours.

For the little fir, it was a whole new world outside of the greenhouse.

For the first time, he saw blue sky, clouds, a warm sun, grass, and trees with leaves.

It felt so good to have the wind blowing through his limbs.

His excitement increased when the truck drove through the arched entry gates of The Happy Valley Christmas Tree Farms.

Located on an expanse of rolling hills, the farm covered hundreds of acres.

Evergreens from seedlings to majestic trees, some over twenty feet high dominated the hills as far as he could see.

Awed by the rolling hills of green, all the little firs could think was, *"We're going to be Christmas trees."*

They could not **believe it.**

5
LIFE ON THE FARM

The seedling firs were planted in long straight rows. To allow for growth, the trees were planted five feet apart.

This would be the little seedlings home for the next ten to eleven years. The little seedling was very comfortable in his new location. The fertile soil felt good around his roots. The sunshine was warm on his branches and needles. The occasional rains were refreshing, and his view of the valley was beautiful.

Bordering the little firs were expanses of more mature firs. Those trees must have been seven years old or more, and were about four feet high.

The little fir liked being planted near the taller trees. He talked to them often.

"When are we actually called a Christmas tree?"

"Where will we be sent?"

"What type of decorations will be placed on us?"

The questions went on and on.

The little fir became increasingly excited, anticipating his future.

6
HARVEST OPERATIONS

On a cold November morning, activity at The Happy Valley Christmas Tree Farms increased dramatically.

A long flatbed truck with several tree-farm workers drove to an area where the fir trees ranged from six to seven feet tall.

Two workers moved rapidly between the rows of stately firs. Working as a team they cut down tree after tree at the trunk base.

The other workers inserted the fallen trees, one at time, through an orange-colored machine that pulled a netted bag over the entire tree. The open end of the bag was tied shut.

The compacted and bagged trees were stacked horizontally on the truck's bed. Hundreds of trees went through the same process.

After loading, the bundled fir trees were strapped into place and the truck was driven away.

For the tiny fir trees, this was their first Christmas season away from the nursery. They all looked on with interest and some concern.

One little fir spoke. "They all looked happy being chosen. I wonder where they are going?" he questioned.

Another small fir chimed in, "It must hurt to be cut down, stuffed into a bag, and stacked on top of one another." The little fir quickly responded, "***Nay***, when you're a Christmas tree, ***that*** doesn't bother you."

His response did not sound too convincing.

7
YEAR END NEARS

A week before Christmas, the demand for fresh cut trees slowed to a dribble.

Thousands of prime fir trees had been cut and shipped to the local markets and adjoining states.

The rolling hills of the tree farm now showed many bare spaces. These areas would soon be dotted with new plantings of seedling firs.

The little fir and his siblings had grown a lot since they were transplanted from the nursery.

It wouldn't be right to call them seedlings or tiny firs any longer. They were now young firs that had grown to be a foot or more tall.

The little fir was now a young fir, but he had concerns about his height. Looking up and down the rows at the other young firs, he was about four inches shorter.

"Gotta stay positive. I'll catch up."

"I'll be okay..... I hope," the young fir mumbled to himself.

8
A SPECIAL CHRISTMAS

On Christmas Eve, the air was crispy and cold. A half-lidded moon played hide-and-seek with the low- hovering clouds.

Down in the valley, colored lights from Christmas decorations blinked and flashed randomly. It was beautiful and serene.

The young firs were spending their second Christmas Eve at the farm. They were in for a pleasant surprise. They were about to be serenaded.

In the village below, a church clock struck the eleventh hour. As the last vibrant tone of the bell faded, a low humming sound started among the trees. Gradually the humming blended with thousands of voices, softly and slowly. Although it was only heard by the trees at the farm, the harmony was exceptional.

The words of the Christmas carol, "Silent Night" were sung in English. A small group of mature firs of German heritage echoed the words in German after each line.

Silent night, Holy night.
Stille nacht, heilige nacht,

All is calm, all is bright
Alles schläft; einsam wacht

Round yon virgin, mother and child
Nur das traute hochheilige Paar.

Holy infant so tender and mild
Holder Knabe im lockigen Haar,

Sleep in heavenly peace
Schlaf in himmlischer Ruh!

Sleep in heavenly peace
Schlaf in himmlischer Ruh!

As the melodic tones faded, all of the young firs responded with cheers of appreciation.

"Hoorah! Hoorah! Hoorah!" echoed through their rows.

9
THE SOBERING YEARS

Over the next four years, the young fir tree nearly tripled in size. But, he still didn't grow as fast as others around him.

Two years ago, he was five to six inches shorter than fir trees of the same age. Now there was nearly a foot difference.

The young tree had a gnawing anxiety.
"What's <u>wrong</u> with me?"
"Why am I <u>runt</u>?"
"Will this affect my being chosen as a Christmas tree?"

He had another situation developing that could cause more serious concerns. On the lower portion of his branches was an obvious bare spot. It started as a small opening through his branches. But, in the past few months it had become nearly six inches wide. He had an ***ugly hole*** in his side.

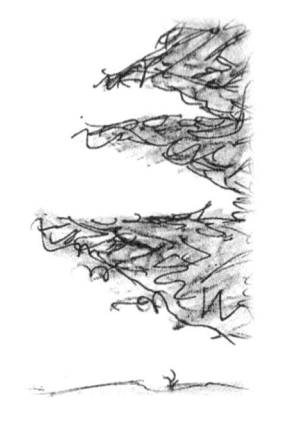

The caretakers were spending extra time trying to correct the young fir's growth problems. This did not stop several trees in the rows near him from becoming verbally abusive.

"Your barn door is open!" they jeered.

"Hey shorty, you have a GAP in your FLAP!" they sneered.

"Close the window – you're letting in the cold air!" they snickered.

The bullying words hurt. But, he tried to turn the slurs into something positive.

The jeering taunt, "You have a GAP in your FLAP", stuck with him.

To counter the cruel verbal attacks, the young tree decided to call himself "Gap". He liked the sound of it. He actually felt comfortable with it.

"I __will__ be a Christmas tree named __Gap__!" he shouted.

10
MATURING

For the next five years, the Christmas Tree Farms of Happy Valley provided thousands of fir trees to the public and commercial markets.

Gap was growing. He was nearing the time of being a candidate for the Christmas tree market.

He remained about one foot shorter than most his age and he now had a dent in his side where the gaping hole used to be.

Most of the trees in Gap's planting area were five and a half to six feet tall. Trees in the six to seven foot range were usually fourteen to fifteen years old.

Gap enjoyed his time at the farm. He found it to be a peaceful and beautiful place to grow up. He also learned interesting facts about his ancestors and the meaning of being an evergreen tree during Christmas.

To Gap, it was mind boggling to learn that over seventy-two million evergreens are grown in the United States each year. Forty million are used for reforestation and landscaping. Thirty million of them are purchased in America as Christmas trees. All of those trees are grown by over twenty-one thousand nurseries and tree farmers.

Gap was proud to be part of this massive program to observe the traditional celebration of Christmas.

11
SILENT NIGHT COUNTDOWN

It had been over eight years since the seedlings were moved to the tree farm. Now, it was Christmas Eve again. They had spent previous Christmas Eves together and they knew this bone chilling night was probably their last as a group.

The air was invigorating under a clear night sky. A full moon cast soft shadows on the rolling hills.

Gap remained quiet. It was sobering to him realizing he probably would not do this ritual again.

After the village clock tolled eleven, the trees sang the traditional "Silent Night." Gap liked this song. He would hum it aloud for weeks after Christmas.

As the last notes faded, Gap choked up and felt a chill go through his branches.

He collected himself remembering the elderly white-haired caretaker at the green house; Gap repeated the caretaker's words, "**Straighten up** little one. *Always* stand tall."

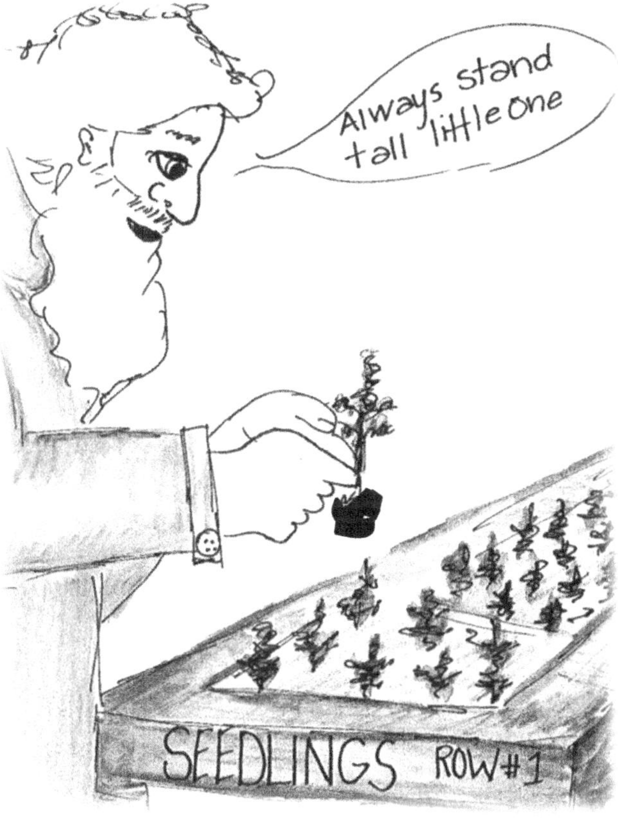
Always stand tall little one
SEEDLINGS ROW#1

12
SPECIAL TREATMENT

One would think they were royalty. The special treatment given to Gap and the maturing trees by the tree farm caretakers was outstanding.

The groomers clipped and shaped the trees' limbs, straightened their branches and supplied nutrients to their roots.

The weather cooperated with plenty of sunshine and refreshing rain. The trees enjoyed the attention.

There were plenty of games being played among their ranks and all the trees were comparing who had the shiniest needles, and the best shape.

Gap felt a big boost in his morale. The individual care made him nearly forget his lack of height and aggravating dent in his lower branches.

For the first time there was a sense of real unity among the trees. They had all come a ***long*** way together and now they were ***so*** close to reaching their goal ------- of becoming *Christmas trees.*

Aside from the attention given to Gap's group, activity continued as usual at the tree farm.

Each month truckloads of new seedlings were brought to the farm to start new plantings.

As the loaded trucks drove by Gap's area, he and the others cheered their arrival.

The seedlings look *so young*, thought Gap.

13
THE PARTING BEGINS

During mid-November, the stillness in the rolling hills was broken by the sound of a large truck. The truck snaked its way up the winding road of the tree farm and parked near Gap's growing area.

Two men in blue coveralls and baseball caps stepped out and opened the rear doors of the truck. An orange colored piece of equipment was unloaded and placed next to the first row of evergreens. A tall tree in Gap's row recognized the machine.

"Hey guys, it's a tree bagging machine.

This is it! This is the day, " he yelled.

Gap's lack of height kept him from getting a clear view.

"It can't be. Christmas is not until next month. It's too early,"

Gap shouted!

A wave of excitement spread up and down the rows of trees. Most of them knew this was the moment they had waited over ten years for. Shouts of glee and happiness rang out over the hills.

"Christmas tree! Christmas tree! Three cheers for the Christmas tree!"

14
SHIPPING OUT

Row after row of trees up to seven feet tall were cut down and neatly inserted into netted bags. After the bags were tied closed, the bundled trees were stacked in the truck.

Gap's row was near the last to be processed. He found being cut down was painless. *The biggest change came when he was no longer standing upright.*

Being passed through the tree- bagging machine was fast. After being inserted into the netted bag, Gap felt his limbs being drawn *tightly* together. It was as if he were *hugging* himself.

Gap was carried and placed near the top of the last row in the truck. He felt lucky not to be on the bottom and have ten to fifteen trees on top of him.

After the truck was loaded, the doors were shut. The trees would not see the light of day again for a while.

A few hours after leaving the farm, Gap had an ***urgent*** need for a drink of water. Since being separated from his roots, he had a burning feeling in his branches and needles. Normally he would consume up to ***three quarts*** of water each day.

Other trees began to call out as they were cramped and thirsty. There was no response. Gradually they became quiet. All they could do was lie there and hear the sounds of the truck tires pounding the pavement.

15
BONDAGE

After what seemed to be an eternity, the truck finally rolled to a stop. The outside temperature warm with high humidity.

Crammed into the cargo space, the trees were extremely uncomfortable and suffering from the heat and an urgent thirst for water.

The truck crew opened the rear cargo doors. The sun was blinding. The trees gradually adjusted to the bright light.

Around them, many cars were parked in rows in a large paved area. Large glass-front buildings circled them and rose high into the sky.

Crowds of people moved in and out of the nearby buildings carrying bags and packages in their arms.

The truck was parked on the outer rim of a shopping mall. A see through wire mesh fence enclosed an area next to the truck. A large sign was atop the fence reading,

"SHOP NOW – FRESH CUT TREES."

When the unloading started, Gap spoke loudly.
"I don't like this. We are going to be in a CAGE!"

16
EXISTING - BARELY

The conditions inside the Christmas tree holding area were challenging. A few display trees were placed in stands with a supply of water in the base. These lucky few drank their fill.

Most of the trees were merely stood upright and leaned against the mesh fence. Some were still wrapped in the bag netting. A few unfortunate ones lay flat on the pavement.

Gap was one of those leaning against the fence. The workers had removed his netting and he was able to stretch out his branches. However, the lack of water was taking a toll on him.

Throughout the day, a thin stream of customers came to look at the trees. A few opted to buy a tree and then rushed off to tie down their purchases on the roof of their cars. Many remarked it was too early to buy a tree and they would be back later.

The day dragged on. The only relief came late in the afternoon when a shower pelted the area. The thirsty trees welcomed the moisture.

Thanksgiving was coming soon. The murmurs among the trees was that would be a *long* weekend and customer *buying* would increase.

The trees were becoming dejected. They needed some hope – some good news – FAST!

17
GIVE THANKS

On Thanksgiving Day, most of the stores in the shopping mall were closed. A few cars spotted the parking lot. There was a sprinkling of window shoppers.

This was not the case at the Christmas tree lot. Inside the mesh fencing, workers hurried about preparing for the big shopping days starting early tomorrow and throughout the weekend.

The trees were surprised and glad to get the stands with a water supply. Trees were removed from the netted bags and set up vertically in the tree stands. They drank their fill of water.

Gap and the other trees became more relaxed. There was a revived spirit growing amid their ranks. Their pleasant conversation and laughter were welcome sounds.

Within the tree lot, a tent was erected to flock trees in different colors.

Near the entry, tables were arranged to provide apple cider, coffee, hot chocolate, and candy canes to the customers.

Today was a day for thanks. The anticipation of a busy tomorrow was a reason for promise and hope.

18
BUSY DAY

It was the day after Thanksgiving; the long weekend, the biggest pre-Christmas shopping day of the year.

Shoppers jammed the malls; traffic crowded the parking lots. The weather cooperated.

The Christmas tree lot was flooded with customers. Many trees were being sold and taken home to be decorated.

Gap and the other tress were amazed at the activity. One by one, the trees around Gap were chosen and hauled away.

A few customers looked at Gap but decided they wanted a taller tree with more limbs.

Some trees were chosen to be flocked and came out of the flocking tent looking beautiful. Customers selected colors of blue, pink and even purple. The most common choice was white to resemble a covering of frost and snow.

Suddenly, a young couple selected Gap to be flocked in white. He was *excited* to be chosen. However, his joy was short lived. The couple changed their minds and chose a ***different*** tree ---- a ***taller*** tree.

In the evening, under the lights, workers moved Gap and a few other trees into different positions for their best showing.

All Gap could do was hope that Saturday and Sunday would be better. Maybe one of *those* days would be his time to be chosen.

19
THE TIME FACTOR

Time wound down heading into Christmas. Despite days with heavy rain showers, shoppers still turned out in droves.

At the Christmas tree lot, good sales volume over the long Thanksgiving weekend reduced the tree inventory.

There was a lot more space between the remaining trees. With repeated customer rejections, Gap felt dejected. Time was running out. His entire life was devoted to becoming a Christmas tree and bringing joy and happiness to a family during this special season.

For days he watched other trees in the lot being chosen. They seemed so happy. He **ached** to share that experience.

In the last few days, Gap started doubting his desire to even be a Christmas tree.

He knew the choice really wasn't his. If he had had a yellow instead of orange label on his tray at the seedling nursery, he would be in a different situation today.

If so, he would be living on some mountainside for the next fifty to eighty years. Maybe being a telephone or light pole wouldn't be so bad. The other options could be pieces of lumber, part of a log cabin, or a paper product.

But, it *wasn't* meant to be.

"*Maybe* I'll be picked to be a Christmas tree later today ---- *or maybe* tomorrow," he uttered sadly.

20
A DARK DAY

The day before Christmas Eve started with a gray overcast sky. By mid-morning a drizzle gradually grew to a steady down pour.

Large puddles formed on the parking lot. A few brave shoppers huddled under umbrellas and rushed toward shelter in the mall.

Over at the Christmas tree lot, attendants stood quietly under a canopy and watched the rain drops form circles on the pools in front of them. Only a dribble of customers came into the lot.

The rain pelted Gap's branches and needles. Normally, a good soaking would be welcomed but, today was different.

Coupled with foul weather and lack of activity, Gap had a bad feeling growing inside. He would find out why very soon.

Shortly after lunch time, a blue pick-up truck stopped in front of the Christmas tree lot.

A tall thin man got out and rushed to find cover beside the attendants. His conversation was direct and brief, "Okay boys, after tonight, let's shut this operation down. Also, get rid of the remaining trees."

Other inaudible words followed.

The trees were **stunned**. They no longer had days to become Christmas trees; it had come down to **hours**.

It began to rain harder and Gap was overcome with emotion. It was **_too_** much. The rain drops dripping off his needles and limbs hid his tears.

21
ON THE CLOCK

Suddenly, it was December 23rd. Less than seven hours were left before the tree lot was to be shut down. With a remaining inventory of less than two dozen trees, the workers moved several trees to outside the mesh fence. Others were spaced farther apart to improve viewing for potential customers.

Gap and six other trees were placed near the back fence facing the entry.

In the first two hours, two trees were sold. At three o'clock the rains started again. Potential customers stayed out of the rain. No sales.

Gap remained sullen and dejected. He recalled his times as a seedling at the nursery and the white-haired elderly caretaker who treated him so kindly.

He also had fond memories of the dedicated workers at the tree farm in Happy Valley. His fondest memory was when the trees sang "Silent Night" on Christmas Eve.

Looking around the Christmas tree lot, Gap wished he had been left at the tree farm for another year or two. He could have grown at least another foot.

The sound of heavy rain interrupted his thoughts. It was six o'clock ---

TWO hours to go.

22
A GIVEN WORD

An hour before closing, the lot workers started dismantling the flocking tent and gathering their gear. Under sagging strings of overhead lights, they moved slowly. Like the weather, everything seemed gray and dismal. The rain, in an off and on pattern, had continued throughout the day.

It was apparent to Gap he was *not* going to be chosen. His earlier enthusiasm and excitement were drained. Gap glanced around the lot at the empty spots where trees had recently stood. Again, he loudly lamented his feelings,

"Why are we still here?"
"Why didn't someone choose us?"

There was *no* response from the other trees. One attendant began bringing the trees outside the fence back into the storage area.

It was when the attendant was carrying the last two trees that he heard a man's voice.

"Hi there. You're not shutting down, are you?"

The attendant turned and saw a tall man in a tan raincoat following a small girl. He noticed she was walking with a limp, and they were both headed toward him. As they neared, the attendant stammered back an answer,

"Yep, we're shutting down tonight until next year."

The man smiled and took the little girls hand and they entered the tree lot.

As he glanced around at the remaining trees, the man spoke, "Excuse me, this is my daughter Mary. We are looking for a nice tree."

Mary stood quietly in her hooded pink rain coat and knee-high red boots. She displayed a shy, infectious smile. The attendant nodded and smiled at her.

He turned and motioned with his hand, toward the remaining trees,

"This is all we have. Sales have been good this year," he said.

The man strolled around the lot and picked out a tall fir. He stood it up in the center of the lot and examined it.

"What do you think of this tree Mary?" he asked while glancing around for his daughter. The little girl had moved and was standing directly in front of Gap.

Mary turned and looked to her father, "It's okay Daddy, but *this one* is different. It's special, I like it," she said firmly while holding on to one of Gap's limbs.

Her father smiled, "Okay, but don't you think it's *too* short? Besides, it has a *big* dent in its side. It's *not full*," he exclaimed.

Gap liked the little girl, but her father's comments were personal and hurt him. A hint of tears formed in Mary's eyes. She turned and limped toward her father.

"Please, Daddy, let's buy TWO trees," she pleaded, "This tree is *special*. I want it... really."

Mary's father smiled again and looked down into his daughters upturned face,

"Honey, we only need *one* tree. Besides, your mother wouldn't understand our buying *two* trees," he explained.

Head down, Mary turned and slowly limped toward Gap. She turned back, and her next comment was a game changer.

"Daddy, this is NOT for us; we could buy *two* trees and *give* one to the homeless shelter in the village."

Mary had uttered a magic word.

The word was "***GIVE***".

Mary's father hesitated and cleared the lump that was forming in his throat.

"Mary, that is so kind. The homeless shelter would certainly appreciate that. I'm so proud of you."

At that moment, Gap would have held his breath and crossed all his limbs if he could.

Gap felt a glimmer of hope that something special was happening.

Embarrassed by her Daddy's praise, a tinge of crimson crept over Mary's face.

One of the lot attendants stepped forward with a broad grin on his face,

"Little girl, you just made my Christmas," he happily exclaimed. Turning to Mary's father he continued, "We've been instructed to dispose of the remaining trees. What better way to do it, than by *giving* them to others. It's perfect, Thank you," he said excitedly.

Mary's father bent down and hugged his daughter, "I love you", he said. "You're so smart!"

Gap watched the developing scene with a glowing hope, "**Stand tall everybody. *This may be very good!***" He yelled with authority to the pensive trees around him.

The two attendants met briefly and conversed. Shortly one spoke. "We're going to donate our remaining inventory to local needy organizations and the less fortunate," he stated.

Turning to Mary and her father he continued, "You and your daughter pick out *four* trees. They are yours at no cost", he said grinning.

Mary's eyes got big. She squealed and clapped her hands. All the trees cheered loudly.

It may have been pure coincidence, but it suddenly stopped raining.

23
A PERFECT SETTING

It was Christmas Eve. The little girl Mary and her parents donated three fir trees to the homeless and childcare center. The center was better known as The Pilgrimage to the locals.

The three trees felt like royalty. They were placed on a raised stage in the large cafeteria.

They stood side by side. Gap was in the middle. They were adorned with lights, strands of threaded popcorn and cranberries and colored paper chains. Holly sprigs, with clumps of red berries, were placed among the tree branches. From the ends of the branches dangled aluminum foil icicles. Each tree was crowned with a silver star.

The cafeteria was crowded with children and needy people.

Village volunteers rushed about welcoming and tending to the crowds. Supporters carried in bags and boxes filled with donated canned and packaged foods, clothes, shoes, coats, blankets, toys and personal effects.

Amid the cheers and the *HO HO HO's,* Santa Claus made a surprise appearance lugging in sacks filled with Christmas stockings. Santa was immediately surrounded by swarms of wide-eyed children. They eagerly reached out for Santa's special gifts of fruits, nuts and candy. The children were filled with joy and excitement.

Once all the children were occupied with their new gifts, "Santa" snuck out the back door. He must have been one of Santa's dependable helpers because when he left, he drove away in a pickup truck.

When the carol singing started, the lights were dimmed except those on the three Christmas trees. A teen-aged girl, with a voice clear as a bell, sang the popular carol, "O' Tannenbaum" in tribute to Gap and his fellow tree friends. The teen received a standing ovation when the song was completed. The three trees cheered in appreciation.

With a piano accompaniment, numerous carols rang out through the building. Before the last carol, hand-held candles were lit.

The last song of the night was "Silent Night". It was the only carol to which the trees knew the words. As the last notes faded, many blessings and hugs were exchanged among all who were gathered in the cafeteria.

"Life is so good. We need to do this every day of the year", Gap said aloud.

24
THE AFTERWORD

AND SO IT CAME TO PASS

Gap and the other two firs were excited at having received the special attention at The Pilgrimage Care Center.

The remaining trees at the Christmas tree lot were also warmly welcomed by other charity groups on Christmas Eve.

The little girl, Mary, was praised by the villagers for helping make it a festive Christmas for so many. But, that is only part of the story. One more important phase was yet to happen. The chain of events that occurred at the Christmas tree lot attracted deserved attention. The local newspaper initiated the story. The news media conducted interviews, and pictures were taken.

An energetic group of villagers developed a program for all the Christmas tree overages at the various vendor lots. They named the program, "*Give a Promise*" with a motto of "*No Tree Left Behind.*"

The public and vendor responses were very favorable and a new legacy was born. Coincidentally, the

"Give-a-Promise" program soon adapted the nick name of "The Gap".

All this, because of a little girl with a limp who appreciated the differences she saw in a stunted, imperfect little fir tree. There seemed to be a lot more smiles, laughter and understanding in the village.

- THE END –

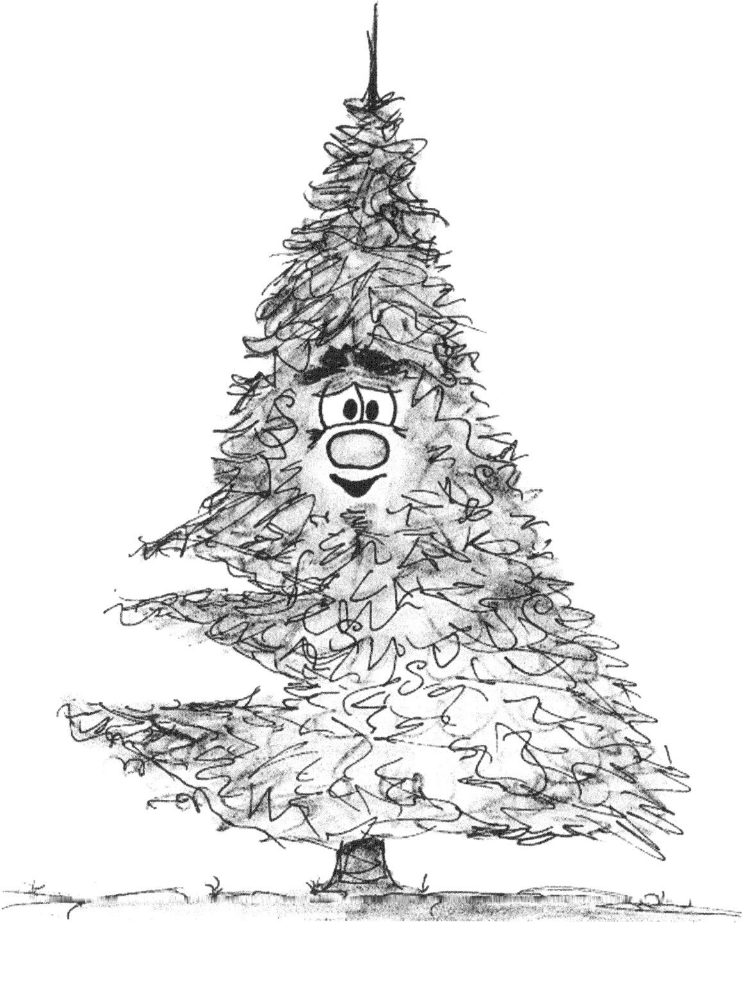

TREE TRIVIA TID-BITS

In the United States, approximately 21,000 nurseries and tree farms produce about 70 million evergreen trees each year.

Of these, up to 40 million are used yearly for reforestation in areas logged off or damaged by forest fires.

The state of Oregon produces the most Christmas trees. The Douglas fir is the State tree.

The state of Washington is called the Evergreen State.

About 25 million evergreens are purchased in the United States each Christmas.

Evergreen Sequoias are located in the Sierra Mountains in Central California at altitudes of 5,000 to 7500 feet.

The oldest Sequoia is named General Sherman. It is over 3,500 years old, 275 feet high with a trunk base and circumference of 101 feet. The trunk is over 37 feet wide.

Sequoia's cousin, the Redwood is among the world's tallest living trees. Redwoods often live thousands of years and may tower over 350 feet in height. Growing along the west coast from Central California to Southern Oregon, the Redwood has fire resistant bark up to 12 inches thick.

Sources: *National Geographic Magazine*, Washington, DC, 20090, 2005-2013

The World Book Encyclopedia, Field, Enterprise Educational Corporation, Chicago, Illinois, 1970

ABOUT THE AUTHOR

From his latest, high powered mystery novel, "Shades of Glass" to a children's book, "The Little Tree That Cried", Clarence Parker provides the reader with a touch of prolific writing.

Clarence told this story of The Little Tree That Cried, to his own children when they were small. Now, decades later they urged him to put this touching story into book form.

Clarence has captured powerful emotions and deep feelings by using trees as the main characters; he hopes that readers of all ages will enjoy this story.

ABOUT THE ILLUSTRATOR

Jimmy Blinn has enjoyed the privilege of working with author Clarence Parker in bringing the story of The Little Tree That Cried into being. Using his God given artistic ability, matched with the writings of Clarence, he allows "Gap" to come to life for the readers.

Jimmy believes this story may likely change the way you look at Christmas trees and perhaps even encourage you to make a difference in someone's life.

Enjoy!

Made in the USA
Columbia, SC
29 November 2023